ARTHUR'S HONEY BEAR

ARTHUR'S HONEY BEAR

Story and Pictures by
LILLIAN HOBAN

Harper & Row, Publishers
New York, Evanston, San Francisco, London

For Eban and Willa Hagerty

It was spring-cleaning day.

Violet was cleaning out

her toy chest.

She made two piles of toys.

One to keep, and one to put away.

Arthur was sticking stamps

into his stamp album.

7

"I am going to clean out
my toy chest too,"
said Arthur. "And I am going
to have a Tag Sale."
"What is a Tag Sale?" asked Violet.

"A Tag Sale is when you sell
your old junk," said Arthur.
"I don't have any old junk,"
said Violet. "I want to keep
all of my toys."

"When I was little," said Arthur,

"I wanted to keep

all of my toys too.

But now I want to sell

some of them."

Arthur began to clean out

his toy chest.

He took a pile of toys
to the back steps.

Arthur took his Hula-Hoop,

his Yo-Yo,

a pile of finger paintings,

and his china horse.

He took his Noah's Ark,

his baby King Kong,

his sand-box set,

his Old Maid cards,

and his rocks and marbles.

Then he took out his Honey Bear.

"Father gave me Honey Bear

when I had the chicken pox,"

said Arthur. "Honey Bear

always tasted my medicine for me

when I was sick."

Arthur moved Honey Bear

behind baby King Kong.

"Now I will make the price tags,"
said Arthur.

"Let me help," said Violet.

"You can cut the paper

for the tags," said Arthur,

"and I will write the prices."

Arthur made a big sign.

It said:

Then Arthur marked the prices

on the tags.

He put tags

on all the toys

and pictures

and rocks and marbles.

"You didn't put a tag

on Honey Bear," said Violet.

"He is in very good shape,"

said Arthur. "He has only

one eye missing.

Maybe I should sell him

for a lot of money.

"Maybe I should sell him

for thirty-one cents," said Arthur.

"His ear is raggedy," said Violet.

"Well," said Arthur, "I have not
made up my mind yet."
He moved Honey Bear
all the way behind baby King Kong.

"Now," said Arthur,

"we have to make arrows.

Then everyone will know

where the sale is."

Violet cut arrow shapes

out of paper.

Arthur wrote "Tag Sale" on them.

Arthur and Violet

hung the arrows on trees.

"Now we will wait for someone

to come and buy," said Arthur.

They waited and waited.

They had some cupcakes and milk.

Violet had a chocolate cupcake

with white frosting,

and Arthur had one

with pink frosting.

Then Norman rode up on his bike.

"How much are the cupcakes?"

he asked. "I have three cents."

"The cupcakes are not for sale,"
said Arthur. "But the rocks
are three cents. So are
some of the pictures."

Norman looked at

all of the rocks.

"I don't see any I want," he said.

Then he tried the Yo-Yo.

"It doesn't snap up," he said.

"Who wants to pay eleven cents

for a Yo-Yo that doesn't yo-yo?"

He picked up the Old Maid cards.

"Only babies play Old Maid,"

said Norman.

"I play Old Maid," said Violet,

"and I am not

a baby anymore."

"This is not a good sale,"
said Norman. "My old toys
are better."
He got on his bike and rode away.

"Here comes Wilma," said Violet.

"Maybe she will buy something."

"Tomorrow is my sister's birthday," said Wilma. "Do you have anything good?"

"Well," said Arthur, "here is a very nice Hula-Hoop."

"It's bent," said Wilma.

"And my sister *has* a Hula-Hoop."

"Here is a china horse," said Arthur.

"How much is the bear?" asked Wilma.

"What bear?" asked Arthur.

"The bear behind baby King Kong," said Wilma. "He doesn't have a price tag."

"Oh," said Arthur quickly,
"he costs a lot."
"Well, how much?" asked Wilma.
"Your sister won't like him,"
said Arthur. "She is too old
for stuffed toys."

"No she isn't," said Wilma.
"She takes her stuffed pig
to bed with her."

"Well," said Arthur, "I will
sell him to you for fifty cents."
"All right," said Wilma.
She took fifty cents
out of her pocket.

"Do you gift wrap?" asked Wilma.

"No," said Arthur.

"Well," said Wilma, "I don't
have money for gift-wrap paper.
If I buy a present
at the toy store,
they will gift wrap for nothing."

36

Wilma put the fifty cents

back in her pocket

and walked away.

Arthur looked at Honey Bear
and hugged him.
He held Honey Bear
and ate the rest of his cupcake.

"I wish someone would buy
something," said Arthur.
Violet said, "I will buy
something, Arthur.
I will buy your Honey Bear."

39

"You don't have any money,"

said Arthur.

"I have thirty-one cents,"

said Violet.

"I can give you

thirty-one cents

and my brand-new

Color-Me-Nice coloring book.

None of the pictures

are colored in yet."

"Well, maybe," said Arthur.

"But maybe I want to keep

Honey Bear for myself."

"I thought you said
you don't want to keep
your old junk," said Violet.
"Honey Bear is not old junk,"
said Arthur. "He is
my special bear."

"I will give you thirty-one cents,
my Color-Me-Nice coloring book,
and my box of crayons," said Violet.
"Only the purple one is broken."
"Honey Bear has been my bear
for a long time," said Arthur.
"He wants me to take care of him."

"I will give you
thirty-one cents,
my coloring book, my crayons,
and half a box of Cracker Jack
with the prize still in it,"
said Violet.
"Well, all right," said Arthur.
So Violet gave Arthur
thirty-one cents,
her crayons,
her coloring book,
and half a box of Cracker Jack.
Arthur gave Violet his Honey Bear.

Arthur took

all of his sale things

and put them away.

46

He put the thirty-one cents

in his mail-box bank.

He ate some of the Cracker Jack.

He read the fortune

on the prize wrapper.

The fortune said:

"Someone you love is gone."

A ring was inside.

Arthur put it on.

48

Then he colored a picture

in his Color-Me-Nice coloring book.

He colored a picture

of a boy holding a teddy bear.

Violet came in

holding Honey Bear.

He was dressed

in a pink tutu.

He was wearing

a necklace and a bonnet.

"Honey Bear is a *boy*!" said Arthur.

"He does not like those clothes."

"Honey Bear is my bear now,"

said Violet. "I will

dress him the way I want."

"You don't know

how to take care of him," said Arthur.

"Well, I am his mother now,"
said Violet, "and I am
taking care of him."

"I think Honey Bear misses me,"
said Arthur. "He wishes
he were still *my* bear."
"Well, he's not," said Violet.
She took Honey Bear for a walk.

Arthur sat down

and ate some more Cracker Jack.

He took the ring,

and put it

on a different finger.

He opened the Color-Me-Nice

coloring book again.

Then he whistled a little tune,

and thought for a while.

Violet came back.

She sat down with Honey Bear.

Arthur thought some more.

Then he said to Violet,

"Violet, are you my little sister?"

"Yes," said Violet.

"Well then,

do you know what I am?"

said Arthur.

"You are my big brother,"

said Violet.

"Yes, I am," said Arthur,

"and do you know

what that means?"

"No," said Violet.

"That means I am Honey Bear's
UNCLE!" said Arthur.

Arthur picked up Honey Bear
and hugged him.

"I am your uncle, Honey Bear,"
said Arthur. "I will always be
your uncle."

"And do you know what uncles do?" said Arthur.

"What do uncles do?" asked Violet.

"Uncles play with their nephews, and they take them out for treats," said Arthur.

"Honey Bear likes treats,"

said Violet. "Can I come too?"

"All right," said Arthur.

Arthur took the thirty-one cents

out of his mail-box bank.

Then he and Violet walked Honey Bear

to the candy store.

Arthur and Violet and Honey Bear

had chocolate ice cream cones.

Honey Bear ate his ice cream cone
on his Uncle Arthur's lap.
"Honey Bear, I am glad
I will always be your uncle,"
said Arthur.

Then Violet and Arthur

helped Honey Bear

eat all of his

ice cream.